THREE NAMES

THREE NAMES

PATRICIA MACLACHLAN

PICTURES BY

ALEXANDER PERTZOFF

A Charlotte Zolotow Book
An Imprint of HarperCollins*Publishers*

Many thanks to Rachel, Adam, and Michael Gaubinger; Randall, Ellika, and David Bartlett; Simon, Sam, Noah, and Amos Girard; and Ann Rundquist, who modeled for me. The book could not have been done without them. And special thanks to Nicholas Gaubinger for his enthusiasm and involvement.—A. P.

Our thanks also to the author's father, Philo Pritzkau, and to her Aunt and Uncle, Jennie and Bill Pritzkau.—P. M. & A.P.

Library of Congress Cataloging-in-Publication Data
MacLachlan, Patricia.
    Three Names / by Patricia MacLachlan ; illustrated by Alexander
Pertzoff.
        p.   cm.
    "A Charlotte Zolotow book."
    Summary: Great-grandfather reminisces about going to school on
the prairie with his dog Three Names.
    ISBN 0-06-024035-0. — ISBN 0-06-024036-9 (lib. bdg.)
    [1. Grandfathers—Fiction.   2. Schools—Fiction.   3. Dogs—
Fiction.   4. West (U.S.)—Fiction.]   I. Pertzoff, Alexander, ill.
II. Title.
PZ7.M2225Tf   1991   90-4444
[E]—dc20   CIP
                                                                AC

Designed by David Saylor
1 2 3 4 5 6 7 8 9 10
First Edition

When my great-grandfather was young—a hundred years ago, he likes to say, but that's not true—he went to school on prairie roads in a wagon pulled by horses. He wore overalls with buckles at his shoulders, and leather high-topped shoes that took a long time to lace—a hundred years, my great-grandfather says, but of course, that is not true either.

His dog with three names went, too.

"How can a dog have three names?" I asked.

"He came to us one day without a name," said Great-grandfather. "My sister Lily called him Ted. Mama called him Boots because his front legs were white halfway up. Papa called him Pal because he was one."

Great-grandfather called him Three Names.

"That's four names," I told him, but he already knew that.

On the first day of school Three Names pranced and danced around the wagon.

"Mama looked me over to make sure I was clean from summer dirt," Great-grandfather said. "Papa kissed me on one cheek and then the other. He smiled at Mama, who went behind the clothesline sheets to cry."

Great-grandfather's mother always cried the first day of school for her own reasons.

Lily drove the wagon because she was the oldest. It was a long way to school, nearly three miles.

"Once we walked."

"Did you get lost?" I asked.

"You couldn't get lost on a prairie road," my great-grandfather told me. "You couldn't get lost with Three Names along to show you the way home."

Three Names liked school. He liked the teacher, Mr. Beckett, who brought leftovers for him. He liked the children, except for William, who was sly.

"Three Names frowned at William," said Great-grandfather.

"I have never seen a dog frown," I said.

"Three Names frowned," he said. "Lily drove the wagon down the road to William's house as Three Names stood in back, his ears up, his tail wagging in circles. The children climbed up in the wagon, laughing; Rachel and Matty and William with their slates and tin pails of lunch. And Three Names always frowned at William."

The wagon rounded the pond; a slough, Great-grandfather called it. The wagon passed fields of prairie grass and wheat, paintbrush and bluegrass, and Three Names barked at what he saw. He barked at the sharp-tailed grouse that flew up, frightened. He barked at the prairie dogs that stood in the fields, their eyes as black as berries.

Once, Great-grandfather told me, Three Names barked at a cloud that covered the sun.

Then, way off in the distance, came the other children, looking small, like tumbleweeds. Martha came on horseback, and Lou on her pony. The Twilling twins, who did not look alike, walked because they lived close by. George and Jenny were already at school, their horses tethered in the fields, eating grass.

"There was a barn, too, for horses, cool and dark, that smelled of hay and harness leather and old wood. It smelled of Jed, Jenny's pinto, gray-dappled Maude, and Sophie with the white blaze face. Mostly," said Great-grandfather, "it smelled the old sweet smell of all the years of horses that had ever slept there."

Great-grandfather's schoolhouse was small and painted white, just one room with wooden desks and a stove and iron hooks on the wall for coats. Three Names slept among the coats and boots and gloves. In winter he slept near the wood stove, thumping his tail when Mr. Beckett opened the door to feed the fire. Sometimes he slept on Great-grandfather's stocking feet, and Great-grandfather felt the beating of his heart.

In the side field there were outhouses, one for girls and one for boys. In winter no one stayed there long. But once, in spring, Lou wrote an entire poem in the outhouse, sitting there, quietly.

Hello you cloud eye windows,
Looking through a blue blanket sky.

All grades were in Great-grandfather's one-room schoolhouse. George was the oldest, and he taught Great-grandfather long division and how to tie his shoelaces in double knots. Matty was only seven,

and when he cried, Great-grandfather put his arm around him and helped him with the alphabet.

"Were there twenty-six letters in the alphabet then like there are now?" I asked.

"Twenty-six, just like now," he told me.

Great-grandfather ate lunch outside in good weather, with cool water pumped from the well for drinking. Three Names drank water from a bowl, and stared into the faces of all the children until they shared their food with him.

Great-grandfather played fox-and-geese in the meadow, and hide-and-seek in the barn, but his favorite game was marbles. He carried his marbles in an old sock and drew a circle in the dust, and everyone took turns. Jenny was the champion, but once Great-grandfather won a pot of marbles. He kept his lucky aggie.

"This aggie is a hundred years old," he said, "like me."

In fall the wind came up, snapping the sheets on the clothesline dry, and the nights were crisp like apples from the root cellar. The horses didn't like the wind, and once they ran so fast that Lily couldn't stop them. She held on tightly, and Three Names didn't bark all the way to school.

In winter the children rode on a sleigh if the snow wasn't too deep. Mr. Beckett rode to school early, before the sun rose, to build the fire to warm the schoolhouse. Some days he roasted potatoes in the stove, and the whole room smelled of warm potatoes and butter from a crock and firewood. Three Names ate a potato, too. All but the skin.

"At winter holidays there was a party at the schoolhouse for everyone," Great-grandfather said, "all the children and parents and grandparents and aunts and uncles. A candle burned in every window of the school. We could see the lights from a long way off, tiny beacons in a sea of snow."

There was food and punch and singing, and Mr. Beckett gave each of them a book for a gift. Martha played her fiddle, and Three Names lifted his head to howl at the rafters.

Spring came and the snow melted slowly. The earth was dark and wet, and the slough filled with water. Sometimes Three Names jumped off the wagon to walk into the slough, lifting his head happily, scaring the birds. There were spring storms, and sometimes tornadoes with thin dark clouds tunneling down from the sky. The children ran to the cellar where it was safe, and Mr. Beckett told stories by lamplight as the wind made a roaring noise all around and Three Names trembled.

"Once, after a storm, we found someone's outhouse behind the barn, blown there by the wind," said Great-grandfather. "Another time Mr. Willeck's old horse Annie appeared, a little mussed, to eat grass with the others."

And then, too soon, it was the last day of school. Spring had turned to summer and dust hung in the air. The grasses had turned snap brittle.

There was a celebration, and everyone came dressed in white starched shirts and calico and shiny shoes.

"I wore new knickers of corduroy that whispered when I walked," said Great-grandfather.

There was lemonade and cookies, and Great-grandfather made Three Names close his mouth so he wouldn't howl when Martha played her fiddle. There was a speech by Mr. Beckett, and one by George because he was graduating.

"I am happy," said George, "but I am sad, too."

"Everyone was sad," said my great-grandfather, "because school was over. Even Three Names was sad, sitting silent in the wagon all the way home, watching the prairie stretched out like a quilt all around."

A hundred years ago when Great-grandfather was young, summer was fine, full of long, warm days, and nights when the moon rose yellow. But he missed school.

"Three Names missed school, too," said Great-grandfather. "Every day he stared down the prairie road. Every day he pranced and danced around the wagon."

And when the locusts buzzed in the summer grass and Great-grandfather lay in the barn hay, Three Names would nudge him with his cool wet nose.

"No, Three Names. Not school time. But soon, I promise," he'd whisper. "Soon."

And Three Names would turn around three times and sigh, settling like a sack of grain beside my great-grandfather, the two of them dreaming away the summer. The two of them waiting for school.